FOR GRAHAM
WiTH LOVE

Copyright © 1991 by Jane Eccles. First published
in Great Britain by ABC, All Books for Children,
a division of The All Children's Company Ltd.
All rights reserved. No part of this book may be
reproduced or utilized in any form or by any means,
electronic or mechanical, including photocopying, recording,
or by any information storage or retrieval system,
without permission in writing from the Publisher.
Inquiries should be addressed to Tambourine Books,
a division of William Morrow & Company, Inc.,
1350 Avenue of the Americas
New York, New York 10019. Printed in Hong Kong

Library of Congress Cataloging-in-Publication Data
Eccles, Jane.    Maxwell's Birthday/by Jane Eccles.    p.  cm.
Summary: For his birthday Maxwell Monster receives a kit for dressing
up like a monster and scares everyone in sight, including himself.
ISBN 0-688-11036-3 (trade)—ISBN 0-688-11037-1 (lib.)
[1. Monsters—Fiction.]   I. Title.   PZ7.E196Max   1992
[E]—dc20   91-16290   CIP   AC

First U.S. edition, 1992
1  3  5  7  9  10  8  6  4  2

# MAXWELL'S BIRTHDAY

# BY JANE ECCLES

TAMBOURINE BOOKS  NEW YORK

**T**his is Paradise Road.

And here is the house where the Monsters live.

This is Mr. and Mrs. Monster with their son Maxwell and his sister Rose. The small one with the bone is Fang, the dog.

Today is Maxwell's birthday.

"Happy Birthday, Maxwell! I've brought
your favorite cereal—Monster Krunch!
And here's my present," said Rose.
"Open it first!"

"Oh, wow! Gummy monsters, jawbreakers, and..." cried Maxwell, digging deeper in the bag, "licorice snakes."

"Look, Rose! Mom and Dad gave me a Walkmonster!" cried Maxwell, opening the present next to his bed.

"There's a gigantic present from Aunt Jane," squealed Rose, pointing to a large package under the bed. "Uh-oh," she added, remembering how Maxwell nearly blew up the garden shed with the Little Scientist Kit Aunt Jane gave him for Christmas.

"It's a Monster Fun Kit! I've always wanted a scary-looking costume," exclaimed Maxwell.

"Let's see what's written on the box! *Complete with fearsome mask, hideous claws, dastardly feet, plus lots of dangling eyeballs.* It's fantastic!" said Maxwell, putting everything on.

"Eek!" shrieked Rose. "It's scary!"

Maxwell growled at her.

"I'm going to show Mom and Dad right away!"

Mrs. Monster was mending a broken vacuum cleaner in the shed. "OH!" she cried, nearly falling off her chair.

"Sorry, Mom. I'll go show Dad."

"Dad, Dad, wait till you see this!" shouted Maxwell, running into the kitchen where Mr. Monster was carefully icing blue swirls on the birthday cake.

"Oh, sorry," apologized Maxwell, as a bloodshot eye plopped in the middle of a swirl.

"I'll just go and show everyone else," said Maxwell.

"Come back!" cried Maxwell, running after his friends.

"Hello, Granny!"

"How repulsive!"

"Come out, Fang.
I won't hurt you.
It's only me!

"Where is everyone?" Maxwell looked around the garden and down the street, but there was no one in sight.

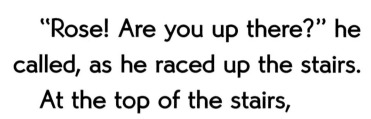

"Rose! Are you up there?" he called, as he raced up the stairs. At the top of the stairs, Maxwell saw a monster in the mirror covered with grotesque lumps, hideous claws, dastardly feet, and lots of dangling eyeballs.

"Aaaagh!" cried Maxwell. He dropped to the floor in shock.

Mom and Dad and Rose heard the bump and ran to him.

"Here's a glass of water, Son," said Dad.

"You look much better, Maxwell," said Mom, as she took off the mask.

"I think I preferred him with it on," said Rose.